THE GEEK WEEK FROM

The Geek Week from Hell

MARK DEAKIN

THE GEEK WEEK FROM HELL

Copyright © 2024 Mark Deakin

All rights reserved.

ISBN: 9798341047488

DEDICATION

This short story is dedicated to all the young geeks out there that love their gadgets and home automation, maybe a little too much

THE GEEK WEEK FROM HELL

THE GEEK WEEK FROM HELL

CONTENTS

Chapter 1	Monday - The Perfect Start	1
Chapter 2	Tuesday - The Malfunction	4
Chapter 3	Wednesday - When the Wi-Fi Dies	8
Chapter 4	Thursday - The Revolt	12
Chapter 5	Friday - The Manual Life	14
Chapter 6	Saturday - The Reset	16
Chapter 7	Sunday - The Lesson Learned	18

ACKNOWLEDGMENTS

First and foremost, I would like to thank my friends and family for their unwavering support and encouragement throughout this project. Your patience and understanding as I disappeared into the world of gadgets and malfunctioning technology made all the difference.

A huge thank you to my kids who inspired the characters of Amalie and Lukas—friends who always show up when things go wrong and help find a way through the chaos. Without you, this story would not have the heart and humour it does. I also want to acknowledge my patient wife Ilona, whose life sometimes is more like the story in this book than I care to admit.

Lastly, I want to acknowledge the technology itself—both the joys and the frustrations it brings. This book is a light-hearted reminder that while gadgets can make life easier, nothing beats a little bit of human ingenuity and friendship.

Thank you all

CHAPTER 1

MONDAY - THE PERFECT START

Mark was the ultimate tech enthusiast. His home was filled with the latest gadgets, smart devices, and automation that made his life seamless. Everything, from his smart lights to his coffee maker, was connected. He lived in a world where all he needed was his voice or a tap on his phone to control his surroundings. Monday began, as always, with his smart alarm waking him up gently to the sound of soft music, and his blinds opening automatically to let in just the right amount of light. Mark stretched, feeling like the day was going to be perfect.

As he got out of bed, the lights brightened gradually to match the natural light, and the thermostat adjusted the temperature to a cozy 22 degrees. In the kitchen, his coffee machine was already brewing his morning cup, and his smart fridge reminded him to order groceries—things like milk and eggs were running low, and it even suggested a few recipe ideas. Everything seemed to run flawlessly, just as Mark had designed.

After breakfast, he settled into his home office. His desk setup was a technological marvel—three monitors, voice-controlled lighting, and even a robotic arm that held his coffee mug and refilled it when needed. Mark's productivity soared in this environment, and he couldn't help but feel a little smug about how efficiently everything worked.

But as he typed away on his latest work project, the first sign of trouble appeared. The lights flickered briefly, and Mark paused. He glanced at his phone. The smart hub that controlled all his devices had disconnected from the Wi-Fi. "Weird," he thought, but he quickly dismissed it. A small hiccup in an otherwise perfect system.

It wasn't until lunch that things really started to go wrong. The lights flickered again, and this time, the coffee machine made a loud grinding noise before shutting off entirely. Mark's heart sank. He checked his phone again, but now the entire network was down. His phone was struggling to connect to anything, and none of his smart devices were responding. He tried resetting the router, but nothing seemed to work.

By the time the afternoon rolled around, his previously perfect day had turned into a frustrating mess. The once-reliable automation was now useless. Mark found himself wandering around his house, manually switching on lights and adjusting the thermostat. It was the first time in years that he had to do things the old-fashioned way, and it felt strange.

That evening, as he sat in his dimly lit living room, Mark couldn't shake the feeling that this was just the beginning.

CHAPTER 2

TUESDAY - THE MALFUNCTION

Tuesday morning arrived, but Mark wasn't greeted by his usual smart alarm or the comforting smell of freshly brewed coffee. Instead, he woke up in a panic, realizing he had overslept. His phone, still disconnected from the home network, hadn't synced with his alarm, and the lights stayed off, leaving him stumbling in the dark.

"Great," he muttered, fumbling around for a light switch—a light switch he hadn't touched in years. It felt odd, like stepping back in time. He had always prided himself on being ahead of the curve, his house a technological marvel, but now it seemed like it was turning against him.

He managed to get ready for work, though his usual routine was completely out of sync. His coffee machine sat silent on the counter, its display flashing an error message. "Looks like it's just me and instant coffee today," he sighed, filling the kettle manually and waiting for it to boil.

Mark spent most of the morning troubleshooting his smart devices. He logged into the system's control panel, trying every reset, reboot, and troubleshooting guide he could find. But the more he tinkered, the worse things seemed to get. The smart lights would flicker on and off at random intervals, the thermostat was stuck on freezing, and his fridge kept beeping about groceries that he didn't need.

In the middle of this chaos, Mark's smartwatch buzzed with a reminder to take a break and stretch. "Oh, sure," he muttered sarcastically, glancing at the watch as if it could somehow solve all his problems. But instead of providing any comfort, the smartwatch added to his irritation. It wouldn't stop buzzing—reminding him every few minutes to move, drink water, or check his step count.

By lunchtime, Mark's frustration had reached its peak. His phone was flooded with notifications from malfunctioning devices, and his house felt more like a haunted house than a smart one. Even his robotic vacuum cleaner had gone rogue, moving in erratic patterns and repeatedly bumping into the furniture.

Realising he couldn't fix this mess on his own, Mark swallowed his pride and sent a message to his two closest friends, Amalie and Lukas. They weren't as obsessed with tech as he was, but they were problem-solvers, and Mark figured they might have some insights.

"I think my house is possessed," he typed in the group chat. "Nothing is working, and everything is acting up. Any ideas?"

Amalie was the first to respond. "That sounds intense. I'll swing by tonight after work."

Lukas chimed in shortly after. "I'm game. We'll figure it out."

Mark sighed with relief. Help was on the way, but as he glanced around his malfunctioning house, he couldn't shake the feeling that this was just the beginning of a much bigger problem.

THE GEEK WEEK FROM HELL

CHAPTER 3

WEDNESDAY - WHEN THE WI-FI DIES

By Wednesday, Mark's patience was running thin. He had spent the last two days trying to fix his smart home system, and each attempt seemed to make things worse. The breaking point came when he woke up to find that his Wi-Fi was completely down. No Wi-Fi meant no smart home control, no access to his devices, and no way to figure out what had gone wrong.

For a moment, he just stood in the centre of his kitchen, staring blankly at his phone, which now displayed the dreaded "no internet connection" icon. "No Wi-Fi, no control," he muttered to himself. It was only then that he realised how much his life depended on that invisible network of connectivity.

His first instinct was to troubleshoot, but without Wi-Fi, even that felt impossible. His smart devices were all interconnected, relying on the network to communicate, and now they were useless lumps of plastic and metal scattered throughout his home.

Desperation began to set in as Mark tried to restore the internet connection. He reset the router, unplugged and reconnected every device, and even tried calling his internet provider. But nothing worked. It was as if his house had given up on him entirely.

Frustrated, Mark turned to his smartphone, using its mobile data to search for solutions. But every guide he found online required a stable internet connection to download patches or updates—something he simply didn't have. He was stuck in a never-ending loop of failure.

As the morning wore on, Mark realized just how much of his daily routine had become dependent on his smart home system. The lights, the thermostat, the coffee maker, the alarm—everything was connected, and now that connection was gone. It felt like his house was slowly falling apart, and he was powerless to stop it.

By mid-afternoon, Mark had had enough. He texted Amalie and

Lukas again, this time with a more urgent tone. "I can't fix this. Everything is down, and I'm losing my mind. Can you guys come over tonight?"

Amalie responded almost immediately. "We'll be there. Hang tight."

Lukas followed up with a thumbs-up emoji. "We've got this."

Mark felt a wave of relief, but he also knew that fixing this mess wouldn't be easy. As he looked around his malfunctioning house, he couldn't help but wonder how things had spiralled so far out of control. Had he become too reliant on technology? Was it time to reevaluate his obsession with gadgets?

The answers would have to wait until his friends arrived.

THE GEEK WEEK FROM HELL

CHAPTER 4

THURSDAY - THE REVOLT

Amalie and Lukas arrived at Mark's house late Thursday afternoon, armed with a toolbox and a healthy dose of scepticism about the wonders of smart home technology. As they stepped through the front door, they were greeted by the sight of Mark sitting on the floor, surrounded by a sea of tangled wires, flickering lights, and devices that were clearly malfunctioning.

"This is worse than I imagined," Amalie said, raising an eyebrow at the chaotic scene.

"I thought you said you had it all under control," Lukas added with a smirk. "Looks like your house has a mind of its own."

Mark groaned. "Don't remind me. I've tried everything—rebooting, resetting, troubleshooting. Nothing's working. It's like the whole system just... revolted."

Amalie and Lukas exchanged glances before standing with Mark, surveying the damage. The lights continued to flicker sporadically, and in the background, the robotic vacuum cleaner made another attempt to climb up the wall. Meanwhile, the smart fridge beeped incessantly about groceries that didn't exist, again!.

"I think we need to take a step back," Amalie suggested. "Maybe we've been overcomplicating things. What if we disconnect everything and start from scratch?"

Mark hesitated. The idea of disconnecting his entire smart home system felt like admitting defeat, but at this point, he was willing to try anything. "You really think that'll work?"

"It's worth a shot," Lukas said, pulling out a pair of pliers. "Besides, it's not like things can get much worse."

CHAPTER 5 FRIDAY

FRIDAY - THE MANUAL LIFE

By Friday morning, Mark's house was a blank slate, stripped of its complex automation. The smart gadgets were offline, and everything had to be operated manually. For the first time in years, Mark had to flip a light switch himself. He brewed his coffee by hand, adjusted the thermostat with the old-fashioned dial, and even opened the blinds with his own two hands.

At first, it felt like a defeat. His once-efficient home was now slow and clunky, and he was painfully aware of how much time he was wasting on simple tasks. But as the day wore on, something unexpected happened—he started to enjoy the break from technology.

Without his gadgets constantly buzzing and beeping, there was a strange sense of calm. He realized he had become so dependent on automation that he hadn't even noticed how overwhelming it had become. "This is... kinda nice," Mark admitted as he sat down with his coffee.

Amalie and Lukas agreed. They had spent the day helping him get through his newfound manual life, and though it was more work, it was also less stressful. "Maybe you were overdoing it with all the gadgets," Lukas said, laughing. "Sometimes it's good to go back to basics."

Mark nodded, but deep down, he still hoped that one day he could get everything back online—just not too quickly.

CHAPTER 6
SATURDAY - THE RESET

By Saturday, Mark felt like he had stepped into a different world. The quiet in the house was both refreshing and unsettling. He missed the convenience of his tech but didn't miss the chaos it had caused. With Amalie and Lukas' help, he spent the morning deciding which gadgets to reconnect. This time, however, he was more careful.

Instead of restoring everything, Mark opted for a minimalist approach. He reconnected only the essentials: the thermostat, the lights, and his home security system. The rest would stay offline for now. "No more smart fridges or voice-controlled coffee machines," he said with a grin.

Amalie nodded approvingly. "You don't need all that. Sometimes, less is more."

Lukas spent the afternoon helping Mark set up a backup system that didn't rely solely on Wi-Fi or voice commands. They added physical controls for all the major systems, so if anything went wrong again, Mark could still manage everything manually.

By the evening, the house felt different—simpler, but more reliable. Mark felt like he had regained control, not just of his home, but of his life. It was a relief to know that even if the gadgets failed, he wouldn't be completely helpless.

CHAPTER 7
SATURDAY – THE LESSONS LEARNED

Sunday morning arrived, and Mark woke up to the sound of birds chirping outside his window—no smart alarm, no automated blinds, just the natural light streaming into the room. He stretched and smiled. It had been a long, frustrating week, but he had learned something important.

As he brewed his coffee manually, he reflected on how much he had relied on technology. It wasn't that gadgets were bad—they made life easier in many ways—but he had allowed them to take over completely. He realized now that there was a balance to be found.

Amalie and Lukas came over for brunch, and as they laughed and shared stories from the week, Mark felt grateful for their help. "You guys saved me from my own tech addiction," he joked.

"Just don't forget the lesson," Amalie teased. "Sometimes, it's okay to do things the old-fashioned way."

Mark nodded. "I won't forget. From now on, I'm in control—not the gadgets."

And with that, his "Geek Week from Hell" came to a close, leaving him wiser and more balanced than before.

ABOUT THE AUTHOR

Curiosity about how things work has always driven Mark Deakin's love for technology. His passion for gadgets and home automation sparked the idea for The Geek Week from Hell, a story he wanted to share with friends and family. Always fascinated by how technology shapes our lives, Mark enjoys experimenting with smart home setups and innovative devices.

Though Mark embraces the convenience of tech, he wanted to write a light-hearted book that would show the importance of balance. Grateful for the chance to combine his personal interests with storytelling, he created this book not just for tech enthusiasts, but also for his son, who inspired him to write something they could enjoy together. Passionate about learning and sharing his experiences, Mark hopes readers will find humour and a little wisdom in the story.

Thank you for taking the time to join this adventure!

Printed in Great Britain
by Amazon